GREAT ILLUSTRATED CLASSICS

THE
JUNGLE BOOK

Rudyard Kipling

adapted by
Malvina G. Vogel

**Illustrations by
Pablo Marcos Studios**

ABDO
Publishing Company

GREAT ILLUSTRATED CLASSICS

edited by
Joshua E. Hanft

visit us at
www.abdopub.com

Library edition published in 2002 by ABDO Publishing Company, 4940 Viking Drive, Suite 622, Edina, Minnesota 55435. Published by agreement with Playmore Incorporated Publishers and Waldman Publishing Corporation.

Library of Congress Cataloging-in-Publication Data

Kipling, Rudyard, 1865-1936.
  The jungle book / Rudyard Kipling ; adapted by Malvina G. Vogel ; illustrated by Pablo Marcos Studios.
     p. cm -- (Great illustrated classics)
  Reprint. Originally published: New York: Playmore: Waldman Pub., 1994.
  Summary: Presents the adventures of Mowgli, a boy raised by wolves and other animals of the Indian jungle.
    ISBN 1-57765-812-4
    [1. Jungles--Fiction. 2. Animals--Fiction. 3. India--Fiction.] I. Vogel,Malvina G. II. Pablo Marcos Studio. III. Title. IV. Series.

PZ7.K632 Ju 2002
[Fic]--dc21

Contents

About the Author

On December 30, 1865, Rudyard Kipling was born to British parents in Bombay, India. His childhood wasn't especially happy, since he was raised by Indian nurses for his first six years, then taken to England to live with a foster family for the next five. He was then sent to boarding school, where he edited the newspaper and began writing.

At age seventeen, Kipling returned to India and spent seven years writing stories and poems for magazines. Many of these, as well as some of his later ones, were based on Indian folk tales told to him by his childhood nurses. Others, especially those involving animals, were influenced by *Aesop's Fables* and the *Uncle Remus* stories. Still others resulted from Kipling's living in England and America, and his travels to Australia, Japan, and Africa.

Kipling's stories and poems for children were very popular. The fifteen stories of Mowgli and his animal friends who appear in *The Jungle Book* (1894) and *The Second Jungle Book* (1895), along with his *Just So Stories* (1902), tell of wise and witty animals whose behavior is very human. They joke, boast, obey and disobey laws, get in trouble and get punished. But they also follow their own animal instincts in order to survive.

Novels, stories, and poems centering around people added to Kipling's popularity. *Kim* (1905) tells the story of a poor orphan's life among the Indian natives. *Captains Courageous* (1897) centers around a rich American boy rescued from drowning by a family of New England fishermen. Kipling's most famous poem, "Gunga Din," recounts the tale of a gallant Indian boy shot while carrying water to British soldiers.

During his lifetime and before his death in 1936, Rudyard Kipling published twelve volumes of short stories, five volumes of poems, and six novels. He was awarded the Nobel Prize for Literature in 1907.

Time to Hunt Again

CHAPTER 1

A Man-Cub for the Wolf Pack

It was seven o'clock on a warm spring evening in the Seeonee Hills of India when Father Wolf woke from his day's rest. "It's time to hunt again," he said as he yawned and stretched.

Mother Wolf lifted her big gray nose from where it had been resting on her four little cubs as they tumbled and squealed before her. She frowned as she said, "Don't forget that Shere Khan is hunting up here in our hills."

"Forget!" began Father Wolf angrily. "That vicious tiger has no right coming up here. The

Law of the Jungle says he's supposed to hunt where he lives, twenty miles away at the Wainganga River. Not only will he scare away all our game for miles around, but he'll kill the villagers' cattle too. Then they'll blame us and hunt us down!"

Just then, the angry whines of a hungry tiger drifted up from the valley below and into the wolves' cave.

"Shere Khan is a fool!" exclaimed Father Wolf. "He's announcing that he hasn't caught anything on his hunt. Does he think our deer are sitting and waiting for him?"

"Hush!" said Mother Wolf. "Listen! He's not whining now. He's purring. That means he's not hunting deer. He's hunting Man!"

"What madness!" said Father Wolf, baring all his white teeth. "The Law of the Jungle declares that Jungle-People may not eat Man because he's the weakest of all creatures. We may kill Man only to teach our children how to kill. And then it must be done far from our

"What Madness!"

own pack's hunting grounds."

At that moment, the tiger's purring grew louder, ending in a howl.

"Shere Khan has missed," said Mother Wolf.

"I can see him from here," said Father Wolf at the mouth of the cave. "That fool jumped in a woodcutter's clearing and burned his feet. Now he's tumbling about in the bushes, muttering and mumbling savagely."

Mother Wolf joined her mate at the cave entrance. "Something or someone is coming up the hill," she said. "We'd better be ready."

As the bushes rustled, Father Wolf dropped to the ground, prepared to leap at whatever or whoever was invading his home and family.

"Wait!" cried Mother Wolf. "It's a man-cub. Look! Bring it here."

Directly in front of them was a little baby who was just learning to walk. He looked into Father Wolf's face and laughed.

Because all wolves are accustomed to moving their own cubs gently, Father Wolf treated

"It's a Man-Cub!"

this man-cub no differently. He closed his jaws on the child's back and carried him to Mother Wolf without leaving a scratch, then laid him down among her cubs.

"How little he is! How soft! And how bold!" said Mother Wolf as the baby pushed his way between the cubs to get at her milk. "What a thing I can boast of now—nursing a man-cub along with my own!"

"He's not afraid of anything, not you, not me, not the cubs," said Father Wolf.

Just then, a roar from the cave entrance announced the arrival of Shere Khan.

"What do you want?" asked Father Wolf quietly, though his eyes blazed with anger.

"The man-cub I was chasing. I forced its parents to run off, and it belongs to me. Give it to me!" roared Shere Khan.

Father Wolf knew that the cave entrance was too small for the huge tiger to fit through, and he shouted back boldly, "We wolves don't take orders from cowardly killers who only

"Give It to Me!" Roared Shere Khan.

attack cattle and cubs. The man-cub is ours—to kill if we choose."

"How dare you talk of choosing! I, Shere Khan, *demand* that cub!"

Mother Wolf sprang away from her cubs and faced the tiger's blazing eyes. "And I, Raksha the Demon, defy you! The man-cub is mine! He shall *not* be killed! He shall live to run and hunt with our wolf pack. And in the end, *you*, hunter of little cubs, *you* shall be the one he hunts! Now go, you cowardly beast with burnt paws!"

Father Wolf knew how strong-willed and shrewd his mate was. And he knew that they were in a better position inside the cave than the tiger was at the entrance.

Shere Khan knew this too, so he backed off, growling and shouting, "We'll see who lives and runs and hunts! We'll see what your pack says about protecting a man-cub. That cub is mine, you bush-tailed thieves!"

Once Shere Kahn was gone, Father Wolf

Mother Wolf Faced the Tiger's Blazing Eyes.

said thoughtfully, "Part of what Shere Khan says is true. We must get the pack's approval before we can accept the man-cub. Are you sure you want to keep him?"

"Keep him!" gasped Mother Wolf. "That poor little cub came here, alone and hungry. Yet he wasn't afraid. That tiger butcher would have killed him, then run away, while the villagers here would take revenge on us! Certainly, I'll keep the cub. See how he's jumping around, like a little frog, like a *mowgli*.... That's what I'll call him, Mowgli the Frog. The day will come, my husband, when Mowgli will hunt Shere Khan just as that tiger has hunted him."

The Law of the Jungle requires that when wolf cubs are old enough to stand, their father must present them to the pack for inspection. Once the cub is accepted, he may run free wherever he pleases.

So, on the next full moon when their cubs were standing, Father and Mother Wolf took

"See How He's Jumping Around."

them and Mowgli to the Council Rock, a hill-top covered with stones and boulders. On this night, over forty wolves had gathered in a circle, while their cubs tumbled over each other in the center.

At the top of the hill, stretched out on a large, flat rock with his head on his paws, lay Akela the Lone Wolf, the strong and cunning leader of the pack. Akela's repeated cries of "Look well, O wolves! You know the Law!" reminded the pack to inspect the cubs carefully.

When Father Wolf decided the time was right, he pushed Mowgli into the center of the circle, where the baby sat laughing and playing with some shiny pebbles.

At that moment, a roar came from behind the rocks, the roar of Shere Khan. "The cub is mine! Give him to me! A wolf pack has no need of a man-cub."

Akela never raised his head from his paws or even twitched his ears as he calmly said, "We do *not* take orders from anyone in the

Over Forty Wolves Had Gathered in a Circle.

jungle except the leader of our pack!"

Forty wolves growled in agreement, except for a brazen four-year-old who asked, "Why does our pack need a man-cub anyway?"

Now, the Law of the Jungle states that if there's any disagreement about accepting a cub, that cub must have two members speak on his behalf. So Akela called out, "Is there any wolf here who will speak for this cub?"

After a long silence, one animal rose on his hind legs and grunted. It was Baloo, the sleepy brown bear who taught all the wolf cubs the Law of the Jungle. Baloo was able to roam freely among the wolves because he wasn't a meat-eater who would take their food. He ate only nuts and honey and roots.

"*I* speak for the man-cub," said Baloo. "He can't do us any harm. Let him run with the pack, and I'll teach him the Law of the Jungle along with the other cubs."

"We need another person besides Baloo," said Akela.

Akela, the Lone Wolf, Leader of the Pack

A huge dark shadow dropped down into the circle. It was Bagheera, the Black Panther. Even though Bagheera had a voice as soft as honey and skin softer than silk, he was a bold, cunning, and reckless jungle hunter.

"I know I have no right to be at your Council meeting," purred Bagheera, "but the Law of the Jungle says that a cub's life may be bought for a price, even by someone outside the pack. Am I right?"

"Yes! Good!" came a chorus of voices. The pack knew that the price would surely be a good meal.

The shrewd Bagheera went on. "Killing that cub now would be a shame, when he might very well be more fun for you to chase when he's grown. So, I'll buy his life with a fat bull I just killed a little way down the hill."

The pack shouted their approval and within moments had disappeared down the hill. Only Akela, Bagheera, Baloo, and Mowgli's family were left at the Rock to face Shere Khan's

Baloo and Bagheera at the Rock of Council

angry roars at losing the man-cub.

"Roar your anger now," mumbled Bagheera, "for the time will come when this man-cub will make you roar in fear! I know this will happen because I know Man!"

"You did well, Bagheera," said Akela. "We know that Man is very wise and this one may help the pack when he's older. One day, my strength will be gone and I'll be killed by the pack. Then they'll need a new leader. Your Little Frog may be that leader."

Akela turned to Father Wolf and added, "Take the man-cub away and raise him as you would your own cub to become one of the Jungle-People."

And that is how Baloo's good words and Bagheera's newly killed bull made it possible for Mowgli to become part of the Seeonee Wolf Pack.

"This Man-Cub Will Make You Roar in Fear!"

Mowgli Grew Up with the Cubs.

CHAPTER 2

Mowgli's Lessons

For the next several years, Mowgli grew up with the cubs. During these years, Father Wolf taught him the meaning of things in the jungle. He taught him to recognize sounds in the grass, smells in the air, scratches of every animal's claws, splashes of every fish, and the language of all the animals in the jungle.

When Mowgli wasn't learning, he sat in the sun and slept and ate. Or he swam in the jungle pools or climbed up into trees for honey, for Baloo had told him that honey was as good to eat as raw meat and Bagheera had taught him how to climb for it. At first, Mowgli clung to the tree trunks, but he soon learned how to swing from branch to branch by watching the apes and monkeys.

Mowgli also learned that he had the power to stare at other animals and force them to look away. He found this to be great fun!

At night, he explored the fields around the villages and peered into men's huts. But after Bagheera showed him traps that men set out to catch Jungle-People, he quickly learned not to trust them.

Bagheera also taught him to swim and run and kill for food. But the panther warned him, "You may kill anything in the jungle that you're strong enough to kill. But you are *never* to kill or eat any cattle because a bull's life paid for your acceptance into the wolf pack. That is the Law of the Jungle."

Baloo was delighted to have such a bright, eager pupil as Mowgli. When he taught the Law of the Jungle to young wolves, they would

He Learned to Swing in the Branches.

learn only what was important to their own pack. But the man-cub had to learn about everything and everyone in the jungle, along with the Laws governing them.

There were many times when Mowgli grew tired of learning his lessons and reciting them back to Baloo, and the bear had to smack him (although very softly). When Bagheera protested (he enjoyed spoiling the man-cub), Baloo insisted, "The man-cub must learn *all* the Laws of the Jungle."

"But the man-cub's head is only seven years old!" argued Bagheera. "It can't remember your hundreds and hundreds of words. Even your smacks and bruises can't force him to!"

"Isn't it better that he's bruised by someone who loves him than to risk his getting badly hurt as the result of being ignorant? I'm now teaching him the Master Words of the jungle. Those words will make him a friend instantly to all the birds, snakes, and four-legged beasts in the jungle. Isn't that worth a few bruises?"

"He Must Learn *All* the Laws of the Jungle!"

The panther had to agree.

"Now, listen, Bagheera. I want you to hear Mowgli recite his Master Words." And Baloo called out, "Come down, Little Brother!"

Mowgli slid down a tree trunk and angrily snapped, "I come for Bagheera and not for *you*, fat old Baloo!"

"That doesn't matter to me," said the old bear. "Tell Bagheera the Master Words you learned today."

Mowgli was delighted to show off, and he boasted, "I know the Master Words for all the languages of the jungle." And the boy spoke in bear language, then switched to bird whistles, then to snake hisses. Proud of his success, Mowgli clapped his hands and jumped on Bagheera's back, gleefully kicking his heels into the panther's side and making the most horrid faces at Baloo.

"Those faces don't bother me," said Baloo proudly. "Some day he'll thank me for all he's learned, for he'll never have to fear any crea-

Mowgli Slid Down.

ture in the jungle."

"Except his own tribe," mumbled Bagheera. Then aloud, he said to Mowgli, "What's all this kicking and dancing on my ribs for, Little Brother?"

"That's what I've been trying to tell you, Bagheera. I'm going to have a tribe of my own and lead them swinging through the trees all day long. They promised me this. And I'll throw dirt and branches at old Baloo!"

"What kind of nonsense are you babbling?" scolded Bagheera.

With his big paw, Baloo angrily scooped Mowgli off the panther's back and onto the ground. "He's been talking with the *Bandar-log*, the Monkey-People!" roared the bear.

Bagheera's eyes flashed with rage. "You ought to be ashamed of yourself, Little Brother! Those gray apes have no Laws and no leaders. Jungle-People refuse to have anything to do with them!"

"But when Baloo hit me, they took pity on

"I'm Going to Have a Tribe of My Own!"

me when no one else cared," sobbed Mowgli.

"Monkey-People don't pity anyone!" snapped Baloo.

"But they were so good to me! They gave me nuts and other good things to eat, and they carried me in their arms up to the top of the trees. They told me I was their blood brother and would be their leader one day."

"They were lying! They have no leader!" argued Bagheera. "They *always* lie!"

"But they were so kind and they invited me to come again. Why didn't you take me to learn from them as you did with the other Jungle-People, Baloo? The *Bandar-log* stand on their feet as I do. They play all day and don't hit me! Let me up, Baloo! I want to play with them again."

"Listen, man-cub!" thundered the bear. "I've taught you the Laws of the Jungle for everyone except the Monkey-People because they are evil and dirty. They boast and chatter and pretend that they're great people. But they're

"Monkey-People Don't Pity Anyone!"

not. They're also cruel. If they come upon a sick wolf or a wounded tiger or bear, they torment him and throw sticks and nuts at him just for fun. Then they shriek and howl and try to get us to climb up their trees and fight them. They even fight among themselves and leave their dead where we can find them. They do everything to make us notice them, but we refuse to. That's why they were so pleased when you came to play with them."

At that moment, a shower of nuts and twigs came raining down on their heads. Bagheera and Baloo took Mowgli between them and trotted off, with the panther warning, "Little Brother, you are to have *nothing* to do with those Monkey-People ever again!"

Actually, the *Bandar-log* didn't want to lose this wonderful seven-year-old leader. They had seen him weave sticks together to make walls and huts, and they wanted him to teach them to do it too. They were convinced that this skill would make them the wisest people

Nuts and Twigs Came Raining Down.

in the jungle and the envy of every creature on land and in the air.

So the *Bandar-log* quietly followed Mowgli and his friends through the jungle. They stayed hidden and watched as all three lay down for their midday nap.

Mowgli was feeling very ashamed of himself as he snuggled on the ground between his two friends. Before he closed his eyes, he made a promise to himself. "I'll never have anything to do with the Monkey-People ever again!"

The *Bandar-Log* Quietly Followed.

Hard, Strong Little Hands Grabbing Him

CHAPTER 3

Kidnapped!

Mowgli wasn't asleep very long when he felt hard, strong little hands grabbing his arms and legs. Then a swash of branches hit his face as he was lifted high into a tree. The next moment, he was staring at Baloo and Bagheera far below him. Baloo was waking the jungle with his deep cries, and Bagheera was bounding up the tree trunk with every white panther tooth bared. But the branches broke under his weight, and he slid down with his claws full of bark.

"Bagheera and Baloo have noticed us!" howled the *Bandar-log* triumphantly. "Now, all the Jungle-People will admire us for our skill and cunning."

Then they began their flight from tree to tree, some fifty to a hundred feet above the ground. Two of the strongest monkeys were clutching Mowgli under his arms as they swung with him through the treetops. The whole tribe followed behind their prisoner, whooping and yelling as they went.

Even though it was a little frightening to see the earth so far below him, Mowgli was delighted with the wild ride at first. But soon, the fear of being dropped replaced his delight. Then his fear turned to anger.

"I must think of a way to let Baloo and Bagheera know where I am," he told himself. "They can't travel as fast on the ground as these *Bandar-log* can through the trees."

With no help possible from below, Mowgli looked up to the sky, where he spotted Chil the Kite. The big hawk was flying over the jungle, searching for some dead beast to eat. When

From Tree to Tree

Chil saw the monkeys carrying something, he dropped closer to see if it could be a meal for him. He whistled in surprise when he saw Mowgli being dragged up to a treetop.

Mowgli remembered his language lessons from Baloo, and he now gave the Kite-Call, which said, "We are jungle brothers, you and I, and I need your help. Mark my trail and take news of it to Baloo of the Seeonee Pack and Bagheera of the Council Rock."

"And what is your name, Brother?" asked Chil.

"Mowgli the Frog. Mark my-y-y tra—il!" And Mowgli shrieked those last words as he was being swung through the air.

Chil nodded and flew upwards, all the while watching with his telescope eyes to see where Mowgli was being taken. "They won't go far," chuckled the hawk. "They never finish what they start anyway. But this time they're asking for big trouble by angering Baloo and Bagheera!"

Chil Dropped Closer.

Meanwhile, the big bear and the sleek panther were trying to follow the *Bandar-log*. But there was no way that their running could keep up with the speedy monkeys as they flew through the trees.

"Chasing them is useless," panted Bagheera finally. "If we follow too closely, they may drop him. We must make a plan."

"They may have dropped him already! You can't trust those Monkey-People. And it's all my fault for not warning Mowgli!" cried Baloo, clasping his paws over his ears and rolling back and forth, moaning.

Bagheera lost his patience. "Enough howling!" he cried. "I have faith in the man-cub. He is wise and has learned much from both of us. Then, too, he has those eyes that stare and frighten the Jungle-People. Perhaps he'll frighten the *Bandar-log* too, even though they don't fear any of us."

"That's it!" cried Baloo, jumping up. "Fool that I am! There *is* one whom the *Bandar-log*

Bagheera and Baloo Tried to Follow.

fear. It's Kaa the Rock Python. That snake can climb as well as they can and he even steals their young ones at night. Yes, we must get help from Kaa."

"But why should he help *us*? He's not one of our tribe."

"Kaa is very old and very cunning and always very hungry. We can offer to hunt many goats for him in return for his help."

So, Baloo and Bagheera set off to find Kaa the Rock Python.

They found Kaa stretched out on a rock ledge in the afternoon sun. He had been away from the other Jungle-People for the last ten days while he was changing his skin. Now, he was admiring his beautiful new coat by darting his head along the ground and twisting his thirty-foot-long body into fantastic knots and curves.

Baloo pointed to Kaa's tongue as it darted over his lips and explained to Bagheera, "He hasn't eaten in many days, so be careful."

Kaa the Rock Python

"Is his bite poisonous?" asked Bagheera.

"No, Kaa's strength lies in his hug. Once his huge coils are wrapped around somebody, they're done for!" Then Baloo called out, "Good hunting, Kaa!"

"Aha, Baloo! Good hunting, Bagheera! What brings you both here? Is there any game nearby to hunt? I need food badly. The last time I went out to hunt in the trees, the branches were too weak to hold my weight. When I almost slipped off, the *Bandar-log* all around me began laughing and calling me the most evil names."

"I know what you mean," purred Bagheera sweetly. "Why, I even heard them say you were an old, toothless, footless earthworm who was afraid to face anything larger than a baby goat! I thought that was terrible!"

The muscles in the old python's throat began to ripple and bulge. This was evidence that Kaa was growing angrier by the minute.

"To answer your question, Kaa, we're here

"I Need Food Badly."

following the *Bandar-log*," explained Baloo.

"I've never known you Jungle-People to be interested in the monkeys," said Kaa.

"We *are* now," explained Bagheera, "but only because they've stolen our man-cub."

"I heard that a man-cub lived with a wolf pack. Is he the one?"

"Yes, and he's the wisest and boldest of all man-cubs," said Baloo. "He's my pupil, and besides, both Bagheera and I love him."

"Our man-cub is a prisoner of the *Bandar-log*," explained Bagheera. "We need your help in rescuing him because you're the only one in all the jungle that these monkeys fear."

"And they have good reason to fear me," said Kaa. "Those foolish, vain *Bandar-log*! But a man-thing in their hands can be in great danger. They can carry a nut or a stick with them for hours, then tire of it and throw it down or break it to pieces. They would do the same to a man-thing."

"That's what we fear," said Baloo.

"They've Stolen Our Man-Cub."

"Where did they take him?" asked Kaa.

"Only the jungle knows," replied Baloo with a shrug. "We think they headed west, toward the sunset. We hoped you might know, O wise Kaa!"

"I? How?" hissed Kaa. "I catch monkeys when they come near, but I don't hunt them."

Just then, a voice screeched above their heads. "Up! Up! Look up, O Baloo of the Seeonee Wolf Pack!"

Baloo looked up as Chil the Kite swept down through the trees. "What is it, my hawk brother?" called the bear.

"Mowgli sent me to tell you the *Bandar-log* have taken him to the Cold Lairs, the monkey city. I've delayed my bedtime to search for you. So, good hunting now, my friends!"

"We thank you, Chil," said Bagheera. "I'll remember you on my next hunt. The head of my first kill will be saved for you, good kite."

"Thank you, Bagheera. The boy knew the Master Word to call to me, and I was glad to

"Mowgli Sent Me!"

be of help. It's the Law of the Jungle."

As Chil flew off, Baloo chuckled. "My little Mowgli remembered the Master Word for the birds, even as he was being dragged through the trees. How proud I am of him!"

"You did a fine job teaching him," praised Bagheera. "But now we must hurry to the Cold Lairs and rescue our little man-cub."

All the Jungle-People knew what the Cold Lairs was—an old, deserted city once occupied by Man hundreds of years earlier. It was now a lost and buried jungle city. Very few Jungle-People ever went there because it wasn't their habit to live in places where Man once lived. Only the Monkey-People lived there now and only when they felt like it, for they had no permanent home.

Baloo looked worried as he explained to Bagheera, "Getting to the Cold Lairs will take more than half the night, even running at full speed. I don't move very quickly, but you know I'll go as fast as I can."

"Now We Must Hurry and Rescue Him."

"We can't take the chance of delaying another minute, good Baloo," said Bagheera. "I know you're just as anxious to get to Mowgli as I am, but Kaa and I can travel more quickly than you. So, we'll go ahead. Just follow us as best you can."

Bagheera sprang away, with the huge python at his heels. Kaa was still enraged over the nasty names the Monkey-People had called him. That, in addition to his hunger, drove him to keep up with the speedy black panther.

Behind them lumbered the big brown bear, running as he never had in his life, for never before was a life Baloo loved in such danger!

Bagheera Sprang Away.

They Ran in and out of the Ruined Houses.

CHAPTER 4

Kaa and the *Bandar-Log*

Even though the *Bandar-log* lived in the Cold Lairs when they felt like it, they had no idea what the buildings or rooms had been used for. They would sit in circles in the king's large council chamber and scratch themselves, looking for fleas.

They would run in and out of the ruined houses in the city, collecting bricks and stones and hiding them for no reason. They would play in the palace garden and shake the trees just to watch the flowers and fruit fall down. They would explore the passages and tunnels in the palace, but never remember what they had seen. They would crowd into the underground tanks to drink the water and play in it until it was all muddy. When they got tired of this, they would return to the treetops and try again to get the Jungle-People to notice them.

When the Monkey-People arrived at the Cold Lairs with Mowgli, they were very pleased with themselves. They had kidnapped the man-cub away from the Jungle-People, and it didn't occur to them that his friends would follow or try to rescue him.

As for Mowgli, the sight of an Indian city, even a ruined one, seemed wonderful. He had never before seen stone buildings, fountains, cobblestone roads, statues, or a palace set atop a hill.

It was late afternoon when Mowgli was dragged into the Cold Lairs and thrown into the center of a circle. The Monkey-People danced around him, singing their nonsense songs and boasting how his capture would

The Sight Was Wonderful to Mowgli.

make them the most important people in the jungle.

By now, Mowgli was sore from his flight among the treetops and angry at his kidnappers. "I wish to eat!" he demanded.

Thirty monkeys hurried away to collect nuts and fruits for him. But they began to fight with each other on the road and soon forgot what they had gone out for.

"Everything that Baloo told me about the *Bandar-log* is true," Mowgli said to himself as he roamed through the empty city. "They have no Law and no leaders, only stupid chatter and thieving little hands. So, if I starve or if I'm killed, it will surely be my own fault. Still, I must try to return to the jungle. Even being beaten by Baloo would be better than being the leader of these ridiculous Monkey-People!"

But no sooner was Mowgli at the city wall than the monkeys surrounded him, pinching him and pulling him back. "You're foolish to try to leave! We're a great and wise and strong

Thirty Monkeys Hurried Away.

and wonderful people!" they boasted. "The most wonderful people in all the jungle! We all say so, so it must be true!"

Surrounded by hundreds of monkeys, Mowgli had to sit and listen for hours to their absurd boasts and idle chatter. As he stared in boredom at the night sky, a large, dark cloud began to move toward the brightly shining moon. "If that cloud covers the moon, it might be dark enough for me to try to run away," he thought to himself.

Meanwhile, that same dark cloud was being watched by Kaa and Bagheera, who had already surveyed the Cold Lairs and were now waiting below the city wall.

"We must be careful," warned Kaa. "The *Bandar-log* are dangerous when so many of them are together. Of course, that's the *only* time they'll fight, when there are a hundred of them against one of us, never when it's one of them against one of us."

"When that cloud covers the moon, I'll go to

Mowgli Had to Listen for Hours.

the terrace where they've got the boy surrounded in a circle," said Bagheera.

"And I'll make my way quickly down the west wall," said Kaa. "Good hunting!"

No sooner had the cloud moved in front of the moon than the black panther raced up the slope and began attacking the monkeys as they sat fifty deep in the circle around Mowgli. There were howls of fright and rage as Bagheera stomped on their rolling, kicking bodies.

Then one monkey shouted, "There's only one of him! Kill him! Kill!"

While a mob of biting, scratching, tearing monkeys jumped on Bagheera, others grabbed Mowgli and dragged him up onto the broken roof of a house. Then they dropped him through a hole fifteen feet down inside it. If he had been a boy raised by men, Mowgli would have been badly bruised by such a deep fall. But he had been well trained in jumping and falling by Bagheera, so he bent his body and

The Black Panther Began Attacking.

landed on his feet.

From the roof, the monkeys shouted down, "Stay here till we've killed your friend! Later, we'll have our fun with you . . . if the Poison-People that live in this house don't kill you first!"

Mowgli could hear hissing and rustling all around him in the rubbish of the ruined house. He quickly gave the Snake-Call. "Sss! We are jungle brothers, you and I."

"Sssss! Sssss!" hissed dozens of low cobra voices. "Sss! Stand still, Little Brother, for your feet could step on us and hurt us."

Mowgli stood quietly in the darkness, listening to Bagheera's deep, hoarse coughs as the panther twisted away, then plunged back into the mobs of yelling and chattering monkeys. For the first time since he was born, Bagheera was fighting for his life!

Mowgli shouted out to his friend, "Roll to the water-tanks, Bagheera! They won't follow you there! Get to the water!"

"Stand Still, Little Brother."

Hearing Mowgli's voice and realizing that the boy was safe gave Bagheera new courage. He was working his way desperately, inch by inch, toward the tanks when a rumbling roar came from the jungle.

"I'm here!" called Baloo. "I'm climbing up the wall! Wait for me!"

The moment the big brown bear appeared on the terrace, a wave of monkeys threw themselves on him. But Baloo stood up firmly on his haunches, spread his paws, and crushed together as many monkeys as he could hold. Then he began to slam wildly at others with his huge front paws.

A crash and a splash told Mowgli that Bagheera had reached the water-tank. Even though the monkeys wouldn't follow him into the water, they surrounded the tank, dancing up and down with rage, ready to attack if Bagheera tried to get out to help Baloo.

While these two fights were going on, Kaa was working his way over the west wall,

Baloo Stood Up Firmly.

coiling and uncoiling himself to be sure that every foot of his thirty-foot body was working. Then he plunged straight down the wall, ready and anxious to kill!

Kaa's first strike was into the center of the mob around Baloo. The mighty python didn't even have to open his mouth or drive his head at them. And there was no need of a second strike, for the monkeys scattered in all directions, screaming in terror, "Kaa! It's Kaa! Run! Run!"

Baloo drew a deep breath of relief. Even with his thick fur, he had been wounded in the fight. Bagheera climbed out of the water-tank once the monkeys surrounding him had also fled, shouting and shrieking.

"Get Mowgli out of that trap!" gasped Bagheera to Kaa. "We have to get away from here before the *Bandar-log* attack again."

"They won't move until I order them to do so," hissed Kaa. And his next hiss spread throughout the Cold Lairs. "Be ssss-still!"

Kaa's First Strike

The monkeys froze in their tracks, and the city became as silent as if it were empty.

"Kaa, we owe you our lives, Bagheera and I," said Baloo.

"Never mind that!" said Kaa. "Where's the man-cub?"

"Here, in a trap," called Mowgli. "I can't climb out."

"Ssss! You'd better get this man-cub out of here," called the cobras inside the house. "He dances like a peacock and might crush our young!"

"This man-cub has friends everywhere," chuckled Kaa. Then he called down, "Stand back, man-cub! Hide yourselves, Poison-People! I'm going to break down the wall."

Kaa slithered around the wall until he found just the crack he needed. Then, after making two or three light taps with his head, he lifted six feet of his body up from the ground and attacked the wall.

It took no more than six powerful, smashing

"I'm Going to Break Down the Wall."

blows to send the stone wall crashing to the ground in a cloud of dust and rubbish. Mowgli leaped through the opening and flung his arms around Baloo and Bagheera.

"Are you hurt?" Baloo asked softly.

"I'm sore and hungry and bruised, but both of you are hurt much worse, my brothers."

"It doesn't matter, as long as *you* are safe, Little Frog," said Baloo.

"I don't know about that," said Bagheera in a harsh voice that left Mowgli a little frightened. "But you realize that you owe your life and this victory to Kaa."

Mowgli turned to find the great python's head swaying a foot above his own.

"So this is the man-cub!" hissed Kaa. "He looks much like the *Bandar-log*. Take care, little man-cub, that I don't mistake you for a monkey some dark evening."

"We are jungle brothers, you and I, O Kaa," said Mowgli. "I owe my life to you tonight, and I swear to give you any food I kill if you are

Mowgli Leaped Through the Opening.

ever hungry."

"I thank you, Little Brother," said Kaa, with his eyes twinkling. "But what can such a bold man-cub hunt and kill that could provide me with food?"

"I've killed nothing yet, I'm too little. But I can drive goats toward my brothers who are hungry. I have great skill in my hands and will repay the debt I owe to you, Kaa, and to Bagheera and Baloo as well."

"You have a brave heart and a polite tongue," said Kaa, as he dropped his head on Mowgli's shoulder. "Now, go along with your friends and sleep. What is about to happen here you need not see."

While Baloo went to the tank to get a drink and Bagheera backed away to put his fur in order, Mowgli stood watching as Kaa glided out to the center of the terrace. The huge python clamped his jaws shut with a loud snap that drew all the monkeys' eyes to him.

"Can you all see me?" Kaa hissed.

"You Have a Brave Heart," said Kaa.

"We see you, O Kaa," came the low, moaning reply from all over the Cold Lairs.

"Then sit still and watch as Kaa does his Dance of the Hunter." And Kaa began a low humming song as he turned in circles on the ground, two times, then three, weaving his head from left to right. Then he slowly began making loops and figure-eights with his body, then soft triangles, then squares, then coils. He never rested, never stopped humming as the night got darker and darker.

By then, Baloo and Bagheera had returned to Mowgli's side. Both animals stood, still as stone, gazing at Kaa and growling low as their neck hairs bristled. Mowgli, too, watched in fascination, not moving a muscle.

Finally, Kaa spoke. *"Bandar-log,* can you move a hand or foot without my orders?"

"N-o-o-o, O Kaa. No-o-o. We cannot move a hand or foot without your orders."

"Good! Then everyone move one step closer to me."

Kaa Does His Dance of the Hunter.

Line after line of monkeys obeyed helplessly. Even Baloo and Bagheera seemed to be under Kaa's spell as they took that same step forward with the Monkey-People.

"Closer!" hissed Kaa.

And they all moved again.

Mowgli grabbed onto Baloo and Bagheera, and pulled them back. The two great beasts were startled, as though they were suddenly awakened from a dream.

"Keep your hand on my shoulder," whispered Bagheera. "Keep it there or I'll be pulled back to Kaa."

Mowgli turned his two friends around and led them, running, through an opening in the wall and out into the jungle. They didn't stop running until they were miles away from the Cold Lairs.

"I'll never come this close to Kaa again!" gasped Baloo, shaking.

"If I had stayed there, I would have continued walking until I was walking down Kaa's

The Monkeys Obeyed Helplessly.

throat," added Bagheera, trembling.

"Many Monkey-People will walk that road tonight," said Baloo. "Kaa will have good hunting."

"But how can all that come from Kaa's just making big, silly circles with his body?" asked Mowgli. "And with a sore nose as well? Ha, ha!"

"That's part of Kaa's powers," replied Baloo. "He can hypnotize his enemies into doing whatever he orders."

"And you'd better not make fun of Kaa's sore nose!" scolded Bagheera. "That nose was sore from saving you, just as my ears and sides and paws are, and Baloo's neck and shoulders as well."

"Don't be hard on him," said Baloo. "It's good to have the man-cub back again."

"Yes, but we've lost many days of hunting, and it's all because this man-cub had to play with the *Bandar-log*."

"It's true," said Mowgli miserably. "I'm an

"Better Not Make Fun of Kaa's Sore Nose!"

evil man-cub. I'm sorry for what I did."

"I know you are, Little Frog," said Baloo. "But the Law of the Jungle says you must be punished even if you *are* sorry."

"I guess I deserve any punishment I get."

Bagheera then gave Mowgli six "love-taps," which wouldn't have wakened panther cubs from their naps; but for a seven-year-old boy, they were a severe beating.

Mowgli took his punishment without a word.

When it was all over, Bagheera said, "Now jump on my back, Little Brother. We're going home."

Mowgli laid his head down on the panther's back and slept so soundly that he never even wakened when Bagheera gently rolled him off onto the floor of his home cave.

"We're Going Home."

"Never Trust Shere Khan."

CHAPTER 5

A Warning for Mowgli

While Mowgli was learning lessons from Baloo and Bagheera over the years, Mother Wolf added her own important one when he was twelve. "You must never trust Shere Khan. He'll always hunt you, and one day you'll have to kill him."

But Mowgli was still young, and young boys forget things as they grow to be teens, things that young wolves never forget.

When Mowgli wasn't busy with his lessons from Baloo and Bagheera, he spent his time with the other young wolves in the pack. In fact, while he seemed to be their leader, he still respected Akela as the leader of the entire Seeonee Wolf Pack and would never go against the old wolf's orders.

But among the Jungle-People, there was one beast who wanted to do just that. It was Shere Khan. The lame tiger had made friends with some of the younger wolves in the pack by letting them follow him for scraps whenever he made a kill. Akela would never have permitted this in his younger and stronger days when he still had control of the pack.

Shere Khan would flatter the young wolves by slyly asking, "How can you fine hunters let yourselves be led by an old, dying wolf and a man-cub? Why, I hear that when you meet at the Council Rock, you don't even dare look into the man-cub's eyes!"

Now, Bagheera had eyes and ears everywhere and knew of the tiger's treachery. He tried many times to warn Mowgli, "Shere Khan is your enemy. He'll try to kill you one day."

Shere Khan Befriended the Other Wolves.

But Mowgli didn't take these or any other warnings seriously. "I have the pack and I have you, Bagheera, and Baloo, so why should I be afraid? Besides, I believe that Shere Khan is all loud talk!"

One day, as Mowgli and Bagheera were deep in the jungle and the boy was lying with his head on the panther's beautiful black skin, Bagheera warned him once again about Shere Khan. This time, though, his words seemed to make an impression on the boy.

"Shere Khan doesn't dare kill you in the jungle because of all those who protect you. But remember that Akela is very old. The day will come soon when he can no longer kill a buck. That day will mark the end of his leadership and his life. Those wolves who accepted you into the pack are old too, and Shere Khan has convinced their children that a man-cub has no place in the pack."

"But I'm no longer a cub," protested Mowgli. "I'm almost a man. Why shouldn't I be able to

Bagheera Warned Him Once Again.

run with my brothers in the jungle? I was born in the jungle, I have obeyed the Laws of the Jungle, and every wolf in the jungle is my brother!"

Bagheera stretched his sleek black body to its full length and gently said, "Little Brother, feel under my jaw."

Mowgli felt under the panther's silky chin and came upon a bald spot.

"No one in the jungle knows that I have that mark. It's the mark of a collar. You see, Little Brother, I was born among men, in the cages of the king's palace, and had never seen the jungle. After my mother died there, I broke the silly lock with one blow of my paw and escaped. Because I had learned the ways of Man, I became more terrible and more feared in the jungle than Shere Khan."

"Everyone in the jungle fears Bagheera, everyone except Mowgli," boasted the boy.

"You are certainly a man's cub, Little Brother. And just as *I* returned to the jungle where

"Every Wolf Is My Brother!"

I belong, so must *you* return to the world of men, where you belong. I only hope you aren't killed by the pack first."

"But why should anyone want to kill me?"

"Look at me," ordered Bagheera, and Mowgli stared at him steadily.

In moments, the big panther turned his head away. "*That* is why," he said. "Not even *I* can stare at you, and I was born among men and I love you. The others hate you because they can't stare back at you, because you're wise, because you're a man!"

"I didn't know any of this," said Mowgli, frowning. "I didn't know they hated me."

"I'm certain that when Akela misses his next kill and the pack turns against him, they'll turn against you too. They'll hold a Council at the Rock and then. . . . But wait! I have an idea!" Bagheera leaped up excitedly and said, "Go down into the valley, to the men's huts. Take some of the Red Flower that they grow in little pots and bring it here."

"So Too Must *You* Return Where You Belong."

By *Red Flower*, Bagheera meant fire, but none of the Jungle-People knew fire by its actual name. They only knew that they lived in deadly fear of it!

Bagheera went on eagerly. "When the time comes, the Red Flower will be a stronger friend to you than either Baloo or I or your wolf family could ever be. Now go, Little Brother! Get the Red Flower quickly and keep it near you at all times."

"I'll go immediately, Bagheera. But are you sure this is all Shere Khan's doing?"

"I'm sure, Little Brother."

"Then I swear by the bull that bought my way into the pack that I'll pay Shere Khan back for this evil!" And Mowgli hurried off.

"My little brother is surely a Man," whispered Bagheera, lying down again. "O, Shere Khan, how you will live to regret that day ten years ago when you went hunting for that little frog we now call Mowgli!"

Red Flower Meant Fire.

Mowgli Was Running Hard.

CHAPTER 6

Forced To Leave the Jungle

Mowgli was running hard toward the village when he passed the stream below his cave and heard the familiar howls of his pack hunting. But he also heard the young wolves bitterly taunting their old wolf leader.

"Show us your strength, Akela! Spring at the buck! Spring if you can, old wolf!"

The snap of teeth followed by a yelp told Mowgli that Akela had missed his prey and had been knocked down by the buck. Mowgli wanted to stop and help his old friend now, but he knew that getting the Red Flower would be a bigger help to Akela later.

"Bagheera was right," he told himself as he ran. "Tomorrow is the day when both Akela and I will be judged by the Council."

It was night when Mowgli came to a hut and peered in through the window. "A Red Flower is burning in the hearth, and the woman is feeding it with black lumps, then blowing on them. I'll wait for my chance to get some."

Mowgli waited outside the window until morning. He saw a man-child put some of the red-hot lumps in a pot and carry it out with him as he headed toward the field to tend the cows.

Mowgli came up behind him, grabbed the pot, and disappeared into the early morning mist before the boy could call for help.

When he was safely away from the village, Mowgli stopped running. He put the pot down and blew into it, as he had seen the woman do. "This thing will die if I don't give it things to eat," he told himself. And he gathered twigs

Mowgli Peered Through the Window.

and dried bark, and dropped them onto the red-hot coals.

As Mowgli headed up the hill, Bagheera came bounding down to meet him. "I bring bad news for you, Little Brother. Akela missed his buck last night. The pack would have killed him on the spot, but they wanted you there too. The Council will meet tonight."

"I was getting the Red Flower, as you told me to," said Mowgli, holding up the pot.

Bagheera peered into it, then drew back. "I've seen men touch a dry branch to those hot lumps and make the Red Flower blossom. Aren't you afraid of it?"

"Of course not!" chuckled Mowgli. "I seem to remember that when I lived with Man, before I was a wolf, I used to sleep beside the Red Flower. It was warm and pleasant."

Mowgli then took the fire-pot up to his cave and spent the day keeping the Red Flower alive. He dipped branches into it until he found one that burned well.

Bagheera Came Bounding Down.

By evening, when he was summoned to the Council Rock, Mowgli was ready.

Akela the Lone Wolf lay by the side of the Rock, no longer on top of it in the leader's position. Shere Khan was strutting about, followed by his gang of young wolves. Mowgli sat down beside Bagheera and placed the fire-pot and branches between his knees.

Then Shere Kahn began to speak, something he never would have dared do when Akela was in full control of the Council.

"He has no right to address the Council," Bagheera whispered to Mowgli.

Mowgli jumped to his feet and took charge. "My brothers, is Shere Khan our leader that he dares speak to us?"

"You no longer have a leader!" snapped the tiger. "Besides, I was asked to speak."

"By whom? By these dogs here?" And he pointed angrily to the young wolves. "Dogs who follow—"

"Silence, man-cub!" howled one young wolf.

No Longer On Top

"Let Shere Khan speak! He has kept our Law."

"No!" thundered several older wolves. "Let Akela speak while he's still alive."

Akela raised his old head wearily and spoke. "O loyal people and even you, young followers of Shere Khan! For twelve years, I've led you on your hunt, and in all that time not one of you has been trapped or harmed. Now I've missed my kill. We all know that it was a clever plot to trick me into it. Still, the Law of the Jungle gives you the right to kill me here on the Council Rock. But it also gives *me* the right to face you, one by one, and fight to the death. So, who will begin?"

There was a long hush among the pack, for no single wolf wanted to face Akela alone.

Then Shere Khan roared, "Bah! Why bother with this toothless old fool! It's the man-cub who has lived too long! He was *my* meat from the beginning, so give him to me and let's be done with this foolishness! If you don't, I'll hunt here forever and you'll starve. Remem-

"The Man-Cub Has Lived Too Long!"

ber, he is just a man!"

"A man! A man!" came shouts from the pack. "Let him go back to his Man-People!"

"No!" shouted Shere Khan. "He'll turn the Man-People against you. Give him to me!"

Akela lifted his head again and said, "The man-cub has lived with us, eaten our food, and driven game for us. He hasn't broken any Law of the Jungle."

"And I paid for him with a bull when he was accepted into the pack," added Bagheera.

"What do we care about a bull we ate ten years ago?" snarled the young wolves.

"What do you care about a promise either?" snapped Bagheera.

"A man-cub can't run with Jungle-People!" howled Shere Khan. "Give him to me!"

"He's our brother in every way except blood," Akela shouted to the pack. "And you would dare kill him? . . . Yes, I see that you *would* dare anything now, since you're all cowards who follow Shere Khan! I know I must die, but

"He Hasn't Broken Any Law."

my life isn't even valuable enough to offer it in exchange for the man-cub's. All I can do is promise you that if you let the man-cub go free, to go back to his own people, I won't bare my teeth against any wolf in this pack. I'll die without fighting and so spare at least three wolf lives."

"But he's a man!" snarled the wolves as most of them gathered around Shere Khan.

Bagheera whispered to Mowgli, "Everything is in your hands now, Little Brother."

Mowgli stood up, with the fire-pot in his hands, and thundered, "Stop all this jabbering and listen, all of you! You've told me enough times tonight that I'm a man, though I've always believed that I'd be a wolf to the end of my life. So, as a man, I can't even call you my brothers. Instead, I call you dogs! And dogs will *not* decide what is to be done to me. *I'll* be the one to decide that! And since I'm a man, I've brought with me Man's Red Flower!"

With that, Mowgli flung the fire-pot on the

Mowgli Stood Up with the Fire.

ground and watched as the red-hot coals lit up some dried moss laying there. The Council drew back in terror as flames leaped up. Mowgli thrust his dead branch into the fire, and as soon as the twigs lit up, he whirled it above his head. The flames forced the cringing wolves to back away.

"You're in control now," Bagheera told Mowgli. "Use that control to save Akela from death. He has always been your friend."

Mowgli nodded and smiled at the old wolf. Then he turned to frown and stare at the rest of the pack. "I'm leaving you dogs, to go to my people. But I'll show more mercy than you have. It's only because I was your brother all these years that I make this promise. I'll never betray you to Man as you have betrayed me here in the pack."

Then Mowgli strode firmly to where Shere Khan sat blinking at the flames. He caught the tiger by the skin on his chin and cried, "Up, dog! Up when Man speaks or I'll set your fur

Flames Leaped Up.

on fire! Open your mouth to speak or bite and I'll ram the Red Flower down your throat!" And he hit the tiger over the head with the red-hot branch.

With Shere Khan whimpering in fear, Mowgli turned back to the pack. "When I return to this Council Rock, it will be to spread out Shere Khan's hide for all to see. As for the rest of you, I order you to let Akela go free, to live out his life as he pleases. You will *not* kill him because *I* say you will not! Now, dogs, leave! You don't deserve to be part of an honorable Council of wolves!"

Then Mowgli began striking right and left with the burning branch, sending the frightened wolves howling from the sparks that landed on their fur.

At last, only Akela, Bagheera, and about ten wolves who had been loyal to Mowgli remained. The boy's knees began to weaken, and a hurt began to grow inside him, a hurt he had never known before. Sobs left his throat and

He Hit the Tiger.

tears ran down his cheeks. These strange hap-
penings in his body frightened him, and he
cried out to Bagheera, "What is this? Am I
dying?"

"No, Little Brother," replied the panther
gently. "These are tears, which only men use.
Let them fall, Mowgli. Let them fall."

Mowgli sat and cried as if his heart were
breaking. He had never cried before in his life.
But then he had never been forced to leave the
jungle before.

After a while, he looked up at his friends and
said, "I'm ready to go. But first, I must say
good-bye to my mother."

Mowgli went to the cave that had been his
home for ten years. He cried against Mother
Wolf's coat, while Father Wolf licked his cheek.

"You won't forget me, will you?" he sobbed to
his Four Brothers, who were howling too.

"As long as we live, as long as we can follow
a trail, we'll always be with you," they
promised. "When you're with Man, come to the

His Home for Ten Years

bottom of the hill and we'll meet you and talk to you and play with you."

"Come soon, O wise Little Frog," said Father Wolf. "Come soon, for your mother and I are getting old."

"Come soon," said Mother Wolf, "for even though you're a child of Man, I've loved you more than I've loved my own cubs."

"I'll come," promised Mowgli, "and when I do, it will be to spread Shere Khan's hide on the Council Rock. Don't let anyone in the jungle forget me. I'll be back."

It was dawn when Mowgli headed down the hill to met those mysterious things called men.

"Come Soon."

He Crossed a Rocky Plain.

CHAPTER 7

Learning the Ways of Man

Mowgli followed the rough road that led down into the valley, running for about twenty miles until he was certain that he was far away from the jungle. He crossed a rocky plain where cattle and buffalo were grazing, then fields of crops. At the far end of the fields stood a little village.

Feeling hungry, Mowgli decided to enter the village. The first man to see him ran shouting for the priest when Mowgli pointed to his mouth to show he wanted food.

Minutes later, a big fat man dressed in white

came toward him, followed by a hundred staring, shouting villagers.

Mowgli tossed his hair back from his face and frowned at the mob. "These Men-People have no manners," he muttered. "They're as bad as the *Bandar-log*."

The priest turned to his people and explained, "There's no need to fear this boy. The white scars on his arms and legs are merely from wolf bites. He's a wolf-child who has run away from the jungle."

"Poor child!" cried one woman to another standing beside her. "He's a handsome boy, Messua. Don't you think he looks very much like your boy who was stolen by that tiger so many years ago?"

Messua stared hard at Mowgli. "He *does* look a little like my Nathoo would if he were alive, but this boy is so thin. No, he can't be my poor lost Nathoo."

The priest knew that Messua's husband was the richest man in the village and that the

"Men-People Have No Manners."

man would reward him for bringing his lost son back. So the priest told Messua, "What the jungle took from you years ago, it now returns. Take the boy into your house, for the gods tell me he is your son."

"I feel as though the pack is looking me over again," Mowgli said to himself. "But if that is what it means to be a man, then I must allow it."

The crowd parted as Mowgli followed Messua to her hut. After she had given him some bread and milk, she placed her hands gently on his head and looked deeply into his eyes. "Is it possible you *are* my son?" she asked. "Oh, my little baby! My lost Nathoo, how I miss him! If the gods told the priest that you are my Nathoo, you shall be my son."

Of course, Mowgli didn't understand anything Messua was saying. He knew only the language of the Jungle-People, not the words of Man. "But, if I'm to live with Man, I must learn to talk like him," he decided.

"Take the Boy Into Your House."

So, just as he had learned to imitate the sounds of all the Jungle-People, Mowgli now began to repeat each word Messua spoke. By the time darkness fell, he had learned the names of most everything in the hut.

Bedtime, however, was a problem. Mowgli was accustomed to sleeping outdoors, and the hut reminded him of a panther trap. So, when Messua closed the door, Mowgli feared a trap and jumped out the window.

"Let him do what he wishes," her husband assured her. "The boy has never slept in a house or on a bed before. If he is truly our son, he won't run away."

Mowgli stretched himself out on some long, clean grass at the edge of the field and was almost asleep when a soft gray nose poked him under the chin.

"*Phew!*" said Gray Brother, the oldest of Mother Wolf's cubs. "I've been following you for twenty miles to bring you news. Wake up, Little Brother."

He Learned the Names of Almost Everything.

Mowgli hugged his wolf brother. "Are all my brothers in the jungle well?"

"All except those wolves you burned with the Red Flower. Shere Khan has gone away to hunt elsewhere until his burned coat grows again. But he swears that he'll return to kill you and throw your bones in the Wainganga River."

"That yellow-striped coward? He doesn't frighten me! Just don't forget to always visit me and bring me news of the jungle."

"And don't let Man make you forget that you're a wolf, Little Brother."

"Man can not make me forget that I love you and the wolves in our cave, just as I'll never forget that I hate the rest of the wolves who cast me out of the pack."

"Remember that you could be cast out of the Man-pack too! Men aren't to be trusted either. But I'll bring you news often. When I come, I'll wait for you among the bamboo trees at the edge of the field."

"That Coward Doesn't Frighten Me!"

Mowgli Was Learning the Ways of Men.

CHAPTER 8

Revenge Against Shere Khan

For the next three months, Mowgli hardly left the village. He was busy learning the customs and language of men.

He had to learn about buying things for money and plowing fields to plant crops. He had to learn to keep his temper and not use his amazing strength on the village children when they made fun of him for not knowing their games or mispronouncing their words.

He had to learn that there were different castes, or classes of people, among the people of India, and that he was not to associate with those of lower castes than his family's. Mowgli found this a difficult thing to remember, so when he helped a low-caste pottery maker pull his donkey out of the mud, the head-man in the village ordered the boy punished. Mowgli had to tend the village cattle and buffalo in the field while they grazed. For a boy who loved being with animals, this was hardly a punishment!

The night before he was to go out with the herd, Mowgli joined the other children in the center of the village under a giant fig tree. They were all sitting around the outside of a circle of old, bearded men who formed a kind of club. Among the men were the village headman, the priest, the barber, and old Buldeo, the hunter.

As the men smoked their big waterpipes, they told wonderful tales of gods and men and ghosts. Buldeo's stories of jungle beasts amazed the children the most, though Mowgli had to cover his face to keep from laughing at

The Circle of Old Men

the old storyteller's lies.

But when Buldeo told his story about the "lame ghost-tiger" who had carried off Messua's son, and claimed that the tiger's body was inhabited by a dead money-lender who had also been lame, Mowgli couldn't keep quiet.

"What ridiculous child's talk that is! The tiger's not a ghost and he limps because he was born lame."

Buldeo was stunned. "Well, jungle brat, if you're so clever and so brave, capture that tiger and collect the reward of a hundred rupees that the government is offering for its hide. But if you can't do that, don't interrupt when your elders speak."

Mowgli got up and turned to go, calling back to the men, "Buldeo hasn't spoken one word of truth about the jungle this whole evening. So how am I to believe his tales of ghosts and gods that he claims he sees?"

Buldeo gritted his teeth in rage as the head-

"Ridiculous!"

man ordered Mowgli to leave the circle.

At dawn, Mowgli climbed on the back of Rama, the great bull, and with a long, polished bamboo stick, he separated the buffalo and the cattle into two herds. He led the buffalo out of the village and down toward the Wainganga River, and ordered the other herd-boys to lead the cattle to their grazing ground.

Once the buffalo had made themselves comfortable in the warm, muddy pools, Mowgli dropped from Rama's neck and hurried toward the bamboo clump to meet Gray Brother.

"I've been waiting here for many days," said the wolf. "Shere Khan returned to our jungle, but game is scarce so he left again. However, he's still determined to kill you."

"Then I'll need you to warn me. If I see you on the big rock outside the village gate, I'll know that Shere Khan is still away. But when he returns, wait for me in the ravine by the orange dhak-tree."

As soon as Gray Brother was gone, Mowgli

Mowgli Climbed on the Back of the Bull.

picked out a shady place and lay down to sleep, for herding is one of the laziest jobs in India. Children who work as herders sleep or sing or weave baskets out of grass or string necklaces out of jungle nuts or build mud castles.

Then, when evening comes, they call the herd together and lead them back to the village.

Many days and weeks went by, with Gray Brother sitting on the big rock and Mowgli lying on the grass while the buffalo basked in the mud and the cattle grazed on the plain. But the day came when the wolf wasn't on the rock. On that day, Mowgli led the buffalo toward the ravine. There, under the orange dhak-tree, sat Gray Brother. Every bristle on his back was standing up in warning, and he was panting breathlessly.

"Shere Khan has been in hiding for a month to keep you off guard. But he followed your trail and is waiting on the slope of the ravine.

Mowgli and Gray Brother

He plans to attack you tonight at the village gate when you return with the herd."

"I'm not afraid of Shere Khan. But tell me, has he eaten today or is he hunting with an empty stomach?"

"He killed and ate a pig at dawn, and drank his fill too."

"Good! That means he's too full to fight or climb up the ravine to escape me. I plan to use the buffalo herd to trap him. But I'll need help separating the herd in half."

"I can't cut the herd in two myself," said Gray Brother, "but I have a wise helper with me." No sooner had he sounded a Wolf-Call than Akela appeared from behind a rock.

"Akela! Akela!" cried Mowgli. "I should have known you wouldn't forget me."

The two wolves ran among the herd and separated the buffalo just as Mowgli ordered, with Gray Brother driving the females to the bottom of the ravine and Akela driving the bulls, with Mowgli leading on Rama, in a wide

The Wolves Ran Among the Herd.

circle to the top. It was a wide enough circle so that they wouldn't give Shere Khan any warning. Mowgli's plan was to trap Shere Khan between the bulls charging down the ravine and the cows waiting at the bottom.

From where he stood at the top, Mowgli saw the steep, sloping sides, where no boulders or trees could give the tiger a foothold if he tried to climb out. "We have Shere Khan trapped now," he told Akela. "I'll tell him we're here."

Mowgli put his hands to his mouth and shouted down into the ravine, "Wake up, Shere Khan, you cowardly cattle-eater!"

Soon, the long, loud, sleepy snarl of a fully fed tiger answered. "Who calls?"

"It is I, Mowgli. Your time has come, you cattle-thief. It's time for me to bring your hide to the Council Rock!" Then he ordered, "Now, Akela! Down! Hurry the bulls down! Down, Rama, down!"

The herd hesitated for an instant at the edge of the slope, but Akela let out a full hunting

"Wake Up, Shere Khan!"

yell and the buffalo pitched over one another, charging down into the ravine. Mowgli, on Rama's back, ran straight for Shere Khan and knocked him down. No tiger, no matter how big and strong he is, can ever hope to stand up against the terrible charge of a herd of buffalo.

After picking himself up, Shere Khan lumbered down the ravine, looking desperately from side to side for a way to escape. But the sides were too steep and he was too full from his dinner to fight. Within moments, the legs of the charging herd were trampling over him.

At the bottom, Mowgli jumped off Rama's back and called to Akela and Gray Brother, "Scatter the rest of the herd or they'll be trampling and fighting each other."

Shere Khan, however, needed no more trampling. He was dead!

Shere Khan Lumbered Down the Ravine.

"It's Over," Said Mowgli Quietly.

CHAPTER 9

Cast Out by Man

"It's over," said Mowgli quietly, as he took out the knife he had been carrying in a sheath around his neck since he had come to live with Men-People.

Even with all of Mowgli's years of training, skinning a ten-foot tiger was no easy job. He slashed and tore and grunted for over an hour while the two wolves held or tugged the skin as Mowgli ordered.

Just as he was bending down to rip off the skin from one front paw, Mowgli felt a hand on his shoulder. He spun around and saw Buldeo glaring down at him. The hunter's large musket was in position to be fired at any moment.

"The herders told us you stampeded the buffalo, wolf-boy!" he raged angrily.

When the two wolves saw the man approach Mowgli, they backed away, unnoticed, waiting to see what would happen.

"And what foolishness are you doing now, trying to skin a tiger!" continued Buldeo. "Oh, I see, it's the Lame Tiger, the one with the hundred-rupee reward for killing him. . . . Well, boy, perhaps I *won't* punish you after all for letting the herd run off. Ha! Ha! Perhaps I'll even give you one of the rupees when I collect the reward for the skin from the government."

"So, you think you can take this skin and claim the reward, do you?" snapped Mowgli. "Well, it just so happens that I have my own plans for using this skin!"

"How dare you talk to the chief hunter of the village like that, you beggar brat! Get up and leave that carcass or I'll beat you!"

The Musket Was in Position to Be Fired.

"I don't have the time or patience to be bothered with you, you old, babbling fool! Come, Akela, this man is annoying me!"

The very next moment, Buldeo found himself sprawled on the grass with a large, gray wolf standing over him.

Mowgli calmly continued skinning the hide, talking as he cut. "Yes, Buldeo, you're right. You won't give me one rupee of the reward because you won't be collecting any reward. There's an old war between this tiger and myself . . . and *I* won!"

Buldeo had truly been a brave hunter all his life, but now he was faced with a wolf who took his orders from a boy. The only way the old hunter could explain it was sorcery, a magic of the most terrible kind! He lay still, barely breathing, half expecting to see Mowgli turn himself into a tiger too. Finally, he got up his courage and spoke.

"Oh, Great King! I'm an old man. I didn't know you were anything more than a herder.

Buldeo Found Himself on the Grass.

Will you allow me to get up, or will your wolf servant tear me to pieces?"

"You may go," said Mowgli, chuckling. "But next time don't interfere with my hunting!"

Buldeo hobbled away as fast as he could, looking back over his shoulder in case Mowgli changed himself into a horrible beast.

It was nearly twilight when Mowgli and the wolves finished cutting Shere Khan's skin away from his body. "We must hide this skin and take the buffalo home," said Mowgli. "Help me herd them, my brothers."

When he approached the gate, half the village was waiting for him. "That's because I killed Shere Khan!" Mowgli said proudly.

But the boy had no way of knowing that when Buldeo had returned, he told everyone a terrible tale of the wolf-boy's magic and sorcery. So now, a shower of stones fell on Mowgli's head, along with cries of "Wolf brat! Sorcerer! Jungle devil!" And that wasn't all.

"Go away!" shouted the villagers to Mowgli.

Half the Village Was Waiting for Him.

"Shoot him, Buldeo! Shoot him!" yelled one man. And a musket went off with a bang, hitting a young buffalo.

"See! He *is* a sorcerer!" cried the priest. "He turned the bullets away from himself and into a buffalo in the herd."

Mowgli was bewildered. "What's going on?"

"They're no different from our wolf pack," said Akela sadly. "They're casting you out too, but they're doing it with bullets."

"Wolf! Wolf!" cried the priest to Mowgli.

"I was cast out of the wolf pack because I was a man, and now I'm being cast out by men because I'm a wolf. Come, my wolf brothers, let's leave this terrible place."

Just then, Messua ran up to Mowgli. "Oh, my son, my son!" she cried. "They say you're a sorcerer who can turn into a beast, but I don't believe that. Still, you must go away or they'll surely kill you. I know you were only avenging my little Nathoo's death."

"You're right, Messua. I'm *not* a sorcerer.

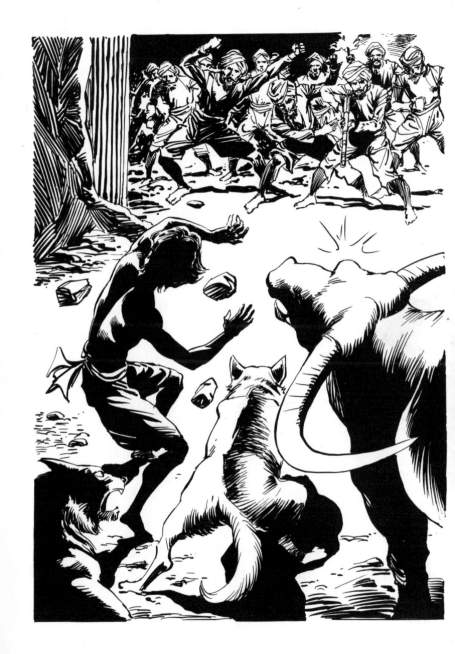

"But They're Doing it with Bullets."

And yes, I *did* avenge Nathoo's death. Now, run back before they begin to stone you too. Go quickly, for I have to send the herd back through the gate."

At Mowgli's command, Akela's yell sent the buffalo charging through the gate, scattering the crowd left and right.

"Farewell, you cruel, evil men!" Mowgli called to the villagers. "You can thank Messua for saving you. If it weren't for her, I'd come in with my wolves and hunt down every last one of you!"

Then Mowgli turned away from the village. "Come, Akela! Come, Gray Brother! Let's get Shere Khan's skin and go away from this place. I've had enough of Man!"

The moon was just going down when Mowgli and the wolves reached Mother Wolf's cave. The boy shouted out, "They cast me out of the man-pack, Mother! But come look! I've returned with the hide of Shere Khan. I've kept my word!"

The Hide of Shere Khan

Mother Wolf walked out toward her man-cub son. "I warned Shere Khan on the day he tried to take you from this cave that you would be the one to hunt *him* one day. You have done well, my son," she said proudly.

"Yes, you *have* done well," came a deep voice from the thicket, and Bagheera came bounding toward Mowgli. "We've missed you, Little Brother! Welcome back, Akela!"

Mowgli, Bagheera, and Akela climbed up to the Council Rock together. Mowgli spread the skin out on the flat stone where Akela used to sit. The old Lone Wolf lay down on it and called his old call to the Council, the same call he had made years ago when Mowgli was first brought there. "Look, look well, O wolves!"

Even though the pack had been without a leader since Akela was overthrown, they answered his call out of habit. Some limped from traps they had fallen into or from gunshot wounds; others were weak and mangy from eating bad food—all things that had never

"You Have Done Well, My Son."

happened while Akela was their leader.

But they came now and saw Shere Khan's striped hide on the rock and the huge claws dangling at the end of the empty feet.

"Look well, O wolves! Have I kept my word?" said Mowgli.

"Yes," bayed the wolves. "Lead us again, O Akela. Lead us again, O man-cub, for we are sick of being without Laws."

"That can't be," Bagheera purred to the pack. "You might turn on them again when your stomachs are full. You wanted your freedom to do what you wished in the jungle and now you have it. You shall hunt alone."

"I, too, will hunt alone in the jungle," said Mowgli sadly.

"No!" said his four cub brothers. "Never alone! We will always hunt with you, today and for all the days to come."

"O Wolves! Have I Kept My Word?"

"Leave Man Alone."

CHAPTER 10

Messua's Rescue

When Mowgli left the Council Rock with Akela and his cub brothers, he returned to the cave to tell Mother and Father Wolf all that had happened to him during his three months with Man, ending with his stoning at the village gate and his farewell to Messua.

"I would have taken my revenge on the man-pack," said Mother Wolf. "Although I would have spared the woman who took you in and cared for you as her son."

"Peace, Raksha!" said Father Wolf. "Our frog has come home again. Leave Man alone."

"Yes, leave Man alone," agreed Baloo and Bagheera, joining them at the cave.

Mowgli smiled. "For my part, I never wish to see or hear or smell Man ever again."

"That may not be possible," said Akela. "As I followed you up here, Mang the Bat flew down and told me that men with guns were seated around a mighty Red Flower in the village. Guns can only mean trouble for us. In fact, Mang said he saw one village man following our trail up to the cave as he flew up to warn me."

"But why?" said Mowgli angrily. "They cast me out. Why would they follow me? What do they want with me now?"

"It's not within the power of Jungle-People to know why men act as they do," said Akela. "*You* are one of them, so it is for you to understand."

Mowgli's hand went for his knife. His eyes blazed with fury as he raged, "Don't ever speak of Man and Mowgli in the same breath,

Mang the Bat Saw Guns.

Akela, or your hide will feel my blade!"

"Enough!" cried Bagheera. Then he jumped up and began sniffing the air.

The wolves then did the same.

"Man!" growled Akela. "Following our trail up from the village! Mang was right."

Mowgli shielded his eyes from the bright sunshine as he gazed down the hillside and noticed something moving in the thicket. "It's Buldeo!" he announced. "I can see the sun's rays flashing off his gun."

Mowgli's four cub brothers began running down the hill in the underbrush.

"Where are you going?" called Mowgli.

"We'll be back with his head for you before mid-day," said Gray Brother.

"No!" shrieked Mowgli. "Come back! Man doesn't eat Man!"

"The man-cub is right," said Bagheera. "Besides, men hunt in packs and others will follow. If we kill this one now, we won't know what the others are planning. Let's wait and

"Enough!" Cried Bagheera.

see what this hunter does."

The four wolf cubs reluctantly came back and sat at Mowgli's feet, waiting for his orders.

"We'll go after him together, my cub brothers," he said, "along with Bagheera."

So, Mowgli and his friends made their way noiselessly through the jungle, circling around Buldeo's path until they had the old hunter surrounded. Mowgli parted the under-brush and saw Buldeo running along, his musket on his shoulder. Suddenly, the old man stopped and stared at the ground. He had lost the trail, which Akela had deliberately mixed up on their return from the village.

Buldeo knelt down and peered at the dirt. "That pack of wolves tricked me!" he wailed angrily. "But I need to rest a while before I try to pick up their trail again."

Buldeo took out his water-pipe and lit it. Soon, his anger left him, and he began to chuckle and talk to himself. "Brave hunter that I am, I know my villagers won't be disap-

Awaiting His Orders

pointed that they sent me out to kill the devil-child who leads the wolf pack. What that boy doesn't know is that we've imprisoned Messua and her husband in their hut and we'll make them confess to witch-craft. Then, once I've killed the boy, we'll burn the parents and take their land and buffaloes! Ha! And I'll get my share too!"

Mowgli translated Buldeo's words for his brothers, although he couldn't understand why Messua and her husband were to be punished. "But Buldeo says the villagers won't do anything until he gets back. So that gives *me* time to get there and rescue those two good people. As for the rest of you, I need you to yelp and howl and frighten old Buldeo until he runs up the nearest tree in fear of his life. Then keep him there long enough for me to get to the village and rescue Messua."

Bagheera and the wolves were delighted to help with the plan. The more they howled, the more Buldeo began running and waving his

"That Gives Me Time."

musket in every direction. The more he ran, the louder they howled. Finally, the old man climbed up a tree to save himself.

Meanwhile, Mowgli was hurrying through the jungle, pleased that his three months in the village hadn't slowed his legs at all. It was twilight when he reached the gate and saw that everyone was crowded around the village tree, chattering and shouting.

Mowgli was glad for the distraction as he crept along the outer wall till he came to Messua's hut. He looked through the window and saw Messua and her husband on the floor, bleeding and groaning. Both were gagged and tied hand and foot.

Mowgli silently jumped in through the window, removed their gags, and cut them free.

"I knew you'd come, my son," sobbed Messua, pulling Mowgli into her arms. "They've been beating us and stoning us all day!"

Mowgli saw her bloody cuts and his whole body began to tremble. "Why do I feel this

His Legs Hadn't Slowed.

way?" he wondered. Then he asked Messua, "Why are they punishing you like this?"

It was her husband who answered angrily. "Because we took you in as our son, they decided we were witches!"

"I don't understand," said Mowgli. "Messua, you explain it to me."

"Because you were my son and because I loved you and raised you, they said I was the mother of a devil and had to die."

"And we're as good as dead already," said the husband gloomily.

"No!" said Mowgli. He pointed out the window and went on. "Out there is the road into the jungle, your road to freedom. Go!"

"We don't know our way through the jungle, as you do, my son," Messua began.

"And the villagers would come after us and drag us back here," added her husband.

"I don't think so," said Mowgli. "They'll have other things to worry about in a very short time. Ah! I hear many shouts from the village

"Because We Took You In."

tree. It seems that my friends have finally let Buldeo come home."

"He was sent out this morning to kill you. Did you meet him?" asked Messua.

"In a way, yes. But now, I want to hear what tale he's telling the villagers. While I'm gone, you decide where you want to go and tell me when I come back."

Mowgli jumped out through the window and ran along the outer wall until he was close to the tree. Stretched out against the trunk was Buldeo, waving his arms at the crowd and groaning as he showed his scraped hands and legs. In between groans, he was telling tales of singing devils who had trapped him in an enchanted tree.

"Bah!" said Mowgli. "Men talk the same foolishness as the *Bandar-log*. And they act foolishly too, listening to all of Buldeo's lies. But their stupidity gives me time to help Messua escape."

Mowgli hurried back to the hut. Just as he

Buldeo Telling Tales

was about to climb through the window, he felt a familiar touch on his foot. It was Mother Wolf.

"What are *you* doing here?" he asked.

"I followed my favorite cub, Little Frog, for I wish to see the woman who saved your life and who helped raise you."

"These villagers mean to kill her and her husband, but I have freed them and will send them on their way through the jungle."

"I'll follow them and protect them. I may be old, but my teeth are still sharp."

"Then wait here, but don't let them see you. It might frighten them." So Mother Wolf backed out into the high grass and hid.

Mowgli swung into the hut again and asked Messua, "What have you both decided?"

"The town of Khaniwara is thirty miles from here. It is governed by the English, who are fair rulers. They don't burn or beat people. They believe in a fair trial. If we can reach Khaniwara tonight, we'll be saved."

It Was Mother Wolf.

"You *shall* be saved," said Mowgli. "But what is your husband doing?" He pointed to the man who was on his hands and knees digging up the earth in one corner of the hut.

The man glared up angrily. "It's my money, you fool! I'll need it to buy a horse. I'm all bruised and can't walk thirty miles!"

"They will *not* follow you. But a horse is a good idea, for Messua is hurt and tired."

Mowgli helped Messua and her husband out the window, then followed behind them. "Do you know the trail to Khaniwara?" he asked.

When they both nodded, he went on. "There is no need to hurry or to be afraid of any voices you hear in the jungle."

Messua smiled at Mowgli and nodded. But her husband snarled, "Well, I'd rather be killed by beasts than by men!"

"Now listen well," said Mowgli in a voice much like the one Baloo used when he was teaching his lessons. "No beast in the jungle will attack you. They will *all* be watching over

The Man Was Digging Up the Earth.

you. I know that *you* believe me, Messua, even if your husband doesn't."

As Messua hugged her son and sobbed, her husband shook his fist and swore, "I'll return one day and bring the law down on the head of every man in this village. I'll get my land and cattle back. I'll have justice!"

Mowgli laughed. "I don't know what justice is, but I don't think you'll see very much left here if you ever do return."

As the two started off into the jungle, Mother Wolf leaped out of her hiding place.

"Follow them!" said Mowgli. "And see to it that all the jungle keeps them safe."

Mother Wolf howled Mowgli's orders through the jungle. When Messua's husband heard it, he turned, as if to run back in fright. But Mowgli shouted cheerfully, "That's only the jungle singing words to protect you. It will follow you to Khaniwara."

"See that the Jungle Keeps Them Safe."

"We Can't Take on the Whole Village Alone."

CHAPTER 11

Letting-In the Jungle

Once Messua, her husband, and Mother Wolf had disappeared into the darkness, Mowgli called Bagheera to him. "I'll need my Four Brothers to help us keep the villagers inside the gate tonight."

"We don't need them," purred Bagheera. "*I'm* strong enough to face any man!"

"You *are* strong, and brave too," whispered Mowgli, stroking the sleek black fur. "But we can't take on the whole village alone. We must devise a plan, for they'll return to the hut soon and find their prisoners gone."

"Let them find *me* in the hut instead!" growled Bagheera. "That should send them all back to their houses and keep them there!"

Mowgli laughed. "You'll have your fun, Bagheera. But I'm not ready to be part of it yet, not until the rest of my plan is set."

The wild yells and rushing footsteps running up the street could only mean that Buldeo's tales were ended and the villagers were coming after their prisoners. Men and women waved clubs, knives, bamboo sticks, and torches as they followed Buldeo and the priest to Messua's hut.

"Burn them!" came the cries.

The crowd broke down the door to the hut and lit up the room with their torches. The sight that greeted their horrified eyes was a huge black panther stretched out full-length on the bed. His paws were crossed and his teeth were bared menacingly.

Everyone froze for a minute, then began to back away, clawing at each other to reach the

A Huge Black Panther Sprawled on the Bed.

doorway. Bagheera raised his head and yawned, then curled his long red tongue toward them, pulling it back only when he snapped his strong jaws together.

By then, the hut had emptied out as the screaming crowd tumbled over one another in their panicky rush to reach their homes. Bagheera then leaped through the window to join Mowgli near the wall.

"They won't leave their huts until daylight," said Bagheera. "What next?"

"Next, I must sleep and then eat."

So Mowgli ran off into the jungle. He slept that night, the next day, and the next night again. When he awoke, Bagheera was beside him, with a newly killed buck at his feet. Once Mowgli had eaten, Bagheera gave him news from the jungle.

"Mother Wolf sent word back with Chil the Kite that the man and woman reached Khaniwara safely."

"Good! And what's happening in the village?"

A Panicky Rush

"The men finally came out of their houses this morning. When they saw me playing near the gate and heard me singing my hunting song, they hurried back inside and shut their doors again. Now that all is well, why don't we get Baloo and go hunting together?"

"Not yet, Bagheera. I'm not finished with those men yet. I need you to find Hathi the Elephant and tell him and his three sons to come here to me immediately."

"*Tell* him? Hathi is the master of the jungle. No one *tells* him what to do."

"With the Master Word I'll give you for him, I assure you he'll come. Just tell him that Mowgli the Frog wants him to come because of *the destruction of the fields of Bhurtpore.*"

"*The destruction of the fields of Bhurtpore,*" repeated Bagheera several times to make sure he wouldn't forget it. Then off he went to follow the man-cub's wishes.

Once the panther was gone, Mowgli began stabbing the earth furiously with his knife.

"I Need Hathi the Elephant."

From the moment he had untied Messua and had seen and smelled her blood, he knew that he had to avenge her beating. Otherwise, the sight and smell of her blood would never leave him. She had been kind to him and had shown him love. He loved her as much as he hated the rest of mankind!

But Mowgli could never dream of killing any man, even one he hated. No, he would get his revenge on the village in his own way!

A while later, Bagheera returned, followed by Hathi and his three sons. "It *was* the Master Word," said the panther, "and they obeyed immediately. Tell me why."

"Hathi is a wise old elephant who once fell into a man-hunter's trap. There, a sharp stake scarred him across his body. When the men came to take him out of the trap, he broke his ropes and escaped.

"After his wounds had healed, Hathi and his three sons came to the fields of the hunters, *the fields of Bhurtpore*, and went on a ram-

Followed by Hathi and His Three Sons

page, trampling all the crops. The land has never been plowed since then, for there's been no one to do it. Everyone fled the village, and the elephants tore every last hut to pieces. No one ever returned."

At this point, Hathi continued the story. "We did the same in four other nearby fields and villages, so that where they once stood, the jungle now grows. We *let-in* the jungle."

"I need the jungle let-in again," said Mowgli. "The villagers who cast me out are cruel and senseless people who kill for the fun of it! They even throw their own people into the Red Flower! I don't want them to live here anymore. I want their village and fields and water trenches destroyed. I want the jungle to grow over everything, so I can smell new grass where I now still smell my mother's blood! Let-in the jungle, Hathi!"

The huge elephant stood before Mowgli, rocking from one foot to the other. Finally, he said, "Even though I have no quarrel with

"We Let-In the Jungle."

these men, your war will be our war, Little Brother. We will let-in the jungle!"

And Hathi turned and led his sons away.

For the next two weeks, the four elephants followed Mowgli's plan and traveled throughout the jungle, each going in a different direction, each spreading the word that they could lead the Jungle-People to better food.

By the end of the second week, they all came together to surround the village and its fields of ripening crops.

It was a dark night when Hathi and his sons came out of the jungle and trampled across the grazing lands and flattened the fields of crops and water trenches. They were followed by armies of wild pigs, deer, and wolves, all rushing to and fro, all eating, all smashing, all trampling, and all fighting in a wild frenzy.

The next morning when the villagers looked at their fields, they saw that their crops were hopelessly lost. That meant no food this season, no grazing land for their herds, and even-

Hopelessly Lost!

tual starvation for them all!

The people stayed on in the village as long as they could survive on what was stored in their huts and on what nuts and berries they could gather in the jungle. But glaring eyes were always watching them from the shadows, and they soon feared straying outside the gate.

In a short while, the rains came and flooded their homes. The people waded out into the mud and finally accepted the fact that their village was doomed!

As the last family hurried out through the gate with their few remaining belongings, they heard the crash of falling beams behind them, then another and another. Hathi and his sons were on a rampage. They kicked backwards at mud walls and tossed doors into the air. They tore through narrows streets and crushed huts left and right until nothing was standing inside the village. It was a repeat of the destruction of the fields of Bhurtpore!

In the midst of this wreckage, Mowgli

On a Rampage

climbed onto Hathi's trunk and said, "The jungle will swallow this all up, my brother, but we must destroy the outer wall too."

With the four elephants pushing, the wall split and fell. The villagers stood outside the wall in the torrential rain, frozen in horror. When they could move again, they dropped their belongings and bits of food, left their few animals, and fled in terror.

A month later, the village was nothing more than a curved hill with soft green sprouts pushing up through the earth. By the time the rainy season ended, a full jungle had grown up on the spot where six months earlier a village had stood and plowed fields had thrived.

The Jungle had been let-in. Mowgli had his victory!

The Jungle Had Been Let-In!

The Years Brought Many Changes.

CHAPTER 12

The Time of the New Talk

The years after the letting-in of the jungle brought many changes to Mowgli's life. Father and Mother Wolf grew old and died, and Mowgli rolled a big boulder against the mouth of the cave so that their death sleep wouldn't be disturbed.

Akela's fur turned from gray to white, and he walked with the stiffness that comes with old age. Throughout this entire time, the Lone Wolf kept urging Mowgli, "Go back to your people, Little Brother. Go back to Man!" In fact, those were Akela's last words before he died. But Mowgli always refused.

It wasn't until two years after Akela's death, when Mowgli was seventeen, that his life was to change again.

Mowgli was still as close as ever to Bagheera, and they spent most of their days together. One spring morning, they woke on a hillside above the Wainganga River. Mowgli sat with his elbows on his knees, looking out over the valley. A strange sense of unhappiness seemed to rise from his toes, travel to his stomach, and fill his chest. Not even the spring songs of the birds or Bagheera's soft purring lifted his spirits.

"It's that time of year again," grumbled Mowgli. "The time when you and the other Jungle-People run off and leave me alone."

"It's spring, the Time of the New Talk," said the panther gently. "There are new voices, new smells, new skins, new rains, new leaves, new flowers. Your Jungle-People go off to find new mates, but return to you with new joy. You've

A Strange Sense of Unhappiness

always loved the Time of the New Talk. Why does it make you sad now?"

"I don't know. I've eaten good food and I've drunk good water. But I've been short-tempered with everyone, even you. I feel hot, then grow cold. Then I don't know what I feel. Perhaps if I go for a long spring run with my Four Brothers, perhaps to the Marshes of the North, I might feel better."

So Mowgli called out a familiar Wolf-Call, but none of the Four answered. They were far away, singing their spring songs with the other wolves of the pack.

Mowgli's sadness turned to anger when he got no reply. "Sure," he pouted under his breath, "when the Red Flower frightens them or when a tiger like Shere Khan hunts them, they run to Mowgli. But now because the Time of the New Talk is here, the jungle goes mad and no one remembers that I'm the master."

Without a word to Bagheera, Mowgli jumped up and ran down the hill into the jungle. He

But the Four Were Far Away.

continued running all that day, stopping only in the evening to eat.

On and on he ran, flying over the land, swinging on vines through the trees, leaping from stone to stone over streams. Running had always made him feel good, and tonight was no different. By the time the moon was high in the sky, he had run forty miles and was feeling better.

When he reached the edge of the marshes, he sat down among the tall reeds to rest. It was then that the sadness returned, but it was ten times worse than before!

"It followed me here!" he cried into the night. And he looked around to see if anything had actually followed him. "I must have eaten poison," he decided. "But no one cares. They sing and howl and seek new mates while I sit here, dying of poison."

Mowgli began to weep at the thought of dying alone. He thought of Akela's death and remembered the old wolf's last words to him

Running Always Made Him Feel Good.

before he died: *Go back to Man!*

"Go back to Man!" shouted Mowgli, jumping up suddenly and frightening Mysa the Wild Buffalo, who had been resting in the swamp.

"I'm sorry if I woke you, Mysa, but I'm new to this marsh. Tell me, is there a man-village near here?"

"Go north!" roared the angry bull. "And don't come back to wake me again, even if you *are* the master of the jungle!"

Mowgli climbed out of the marsh and began to run north. It wasn't long before something shining up ahead made him stop and stare hard. "It's the Red Flower—the kind that grows inside a hut. I remember lying beside one like that before I came to the Seeonee Pack." And he began running harder toward the Red Flower, as if something magical were drawing him to it.

As he approached the lighted hut, several dogs yelped at him, but he silenced them with a deep wolf-growl.

Go Back to Man!

The door to the hut opened and a woman peered out into the darkness. A child inside began to cry, and the woman called over her shoulder, "Go back to sleep, little one. Whatever woke the dogs is gone now."

Mowgli felt himself begin to shake all over, as if he had a fever. He knew that voice well, but he had to be certain. So he called out softly, "Messua! Oh, Messua!"

"Wh-who's calling me?" came a shaky reply.

"Have you forgotten my voice already?"

"If it's really you, tell me the name I gave you!"

"Nathoo! Nathoo!"

"Come, my son! Come to me!"

Mowgli stepped into the light and stared at the woman who had been so good to him. She was older and her hair was gray, but her gentle voice hadn't changed and her eyes still gazed at him with love.

Messua stared at the young man before her. He was no longer the boy she remembered

The Door to the Hut Opened.

from the jungle village. He was strong and tall and wonderfully handsome. "My son, you've grown into a god of the jungle! We all owe our lives to you. But how did you find us?"

"I didn't know you were here. I saw this light and came toward it. Is this the place you called Khaniwara?"

"Yes, my son. The English who rule here wanted to help us against those people in the village. But when we returned with their officials, the village was no longer there. My husband then found work in the fields here, but we don't need much now, we two." And she pointed to a child asleep on a cot.

"And where is the man who dug up his money from your hut?"

"He died a year ago."

"And he?" asked Mowgli, pointing to the sleeping child.

"My son. He was born two years ago." And she picked up the baby, who smiled sleepily and reached out to touch the shiny knife hang-

"A God of the Jungle!"

ing around Mowgli's neck.

Mowgli gently took the baby's hand away as Messua went on. "If you are truly Nathoo, then this baby is your brother."

Mowgli sat down and put his face in his hands. Strange feelings were running through him, making him a little dizzy.

"Oh, you poor boy!" cried Messua. "You've been running through the marshes and are soaked to the skin! You must have a fever. I'll make a fire now and fix you some warm milk."

The warm milk felt good in Mowgli's stomach, but what felt even better was Messua standing over him, patting his shoulder.

"Has anyone ever told you that you're more beautiful than any other man?" she said.

Mowgli looked up, bewildered. He had never heard words like this. But when Messua laughed at his bewilderment, he laughed too.

Soon, the warm milk began relaxing Mowgli after his forty-mile run. He curled up on the floor and in a minute was fast asleep.

"Then this Baby Is Your Brother."

Messua pushed his hair back from his eyes and put a cover over him. Then she was content to just sit and watch her son sleep, which Mowgli did for the rest of that night and all the next day. He was at peace; he knew he had nothing to fear.

When he awoke, Messua fixed a dinner of rice, fruit, and bread. This would fill his stomach until he could hunt for meat.

Mowgli was also anxious to finish his spring run, but the baby wanted to sit in his arms and Messua insisted on combing his beautiful long hair.

Messua sang as she combed, until she heard a wolf whine outside the hut and saw a large gray paw slowly edge under the door. Her jaw dropped open in horror and her hand froze with the comb in mid-air.

Mowgli didn't turn his head at the sound, but simply called out in jungle-talk, "You can wait outside, Gray Brother. You didn't come when I called, so now you can wait!"

Content Just to Watch Her Son Sleep

And the large gray paw disappeared.

"Please don't bring your jungle servants with you, my son. I wish to live in peace."

"You *are* in peace, Mother. All of these Jungle-People, or my servants as you call them, were guarding you the night you came here. They're calling me now. I must go."

Messua stepped aside, as if obeying a god. But the next moment, she was a mother again. She threw her arms around Mowgli's neck and pleaded, "Come back, my son, for I love you. And so does your little brother!"

The child was crying now because the nice man with the shiny knife was going away.

Mowgli suddenly felt his throat close up. Tears filled his eyes as he said, "I *will* come back, Mother. I promise."

As he stepped outside the door, Mowgli called to Gray Brother, "Come, run with me." His voice was as gentle as it had been to the baby as he asked, "Why didn't you Four come when I called you so long ago?"

"I Must Go."

"So long ago? It was only last night, Little Brother. We were in the jungle, and as soon as our songs were done, I followed your trail. But what are you doing with the man-pack in the village we just left?"

Mowgli was about to answer when a beautiful girl in a white dress came down a path leading to the village. Gray Brother hid in the underbrush while Mowgli backed into a field of tall grain. The girl passed close enough for Mowgli to have touched her, but he stayed hidden, parting the tall stalks after she had passed and watching her in fascination till she was out of sight.

"What am I doing with the man-pack?" Mowgli repeated Gray Brother's question when they both came out of hiding. "I don't know. But would you follow me to the man-pack?"

"I followed you on the night our wolf pack cast you out, and I followed you tonight."

"Would you follow me again, Gray Brother?

Close Enough to Touch

And again and again?"

Gray Brother growled as he answered. "You have gone back then? Man goes to Man at last! Our mother said you should, and so did Akela and Kaa."

"And what do *you* say, Gray Brother?"

"They cast you out once with stones. They sent Buldeo to kill you with bullets. They would have thrown you into the Red Flower. You, yourself, have said they are evil. You, yourself, have let-in the jungle on them!"

"And I ask you again what do *you* say, Gray Brother?"

The wolf continued running without answering. Finally, he stopped and said, "Man-cub, master of the jungle, my brother! Although I might forget you for a short time in the spring, your trail is always my trail, your home is always my home, your enemy is always my enemy. I speak for our Three Brothers as well when I say if you go to Man, we will follow you and be with you always!"

"What Do *You* Say, Gray Brother?"

He Found Only His Brothers, Baloo, and Kaa.

CHAPTER 13

Man Goes to Man At Last!

Mowgli sent Gray Brother to summon the pack to the Council Rock to hear his news, but the Time of the New Talk was too important for anyone to be interrupted, even by the master of the jungle.

So it happened that when Mowgli climbed up to the Council Rock, he found only his Four Brothers, old Baloo who was nearly blind, and Kaa, who was coiled around Akela's empty seat.

Mowgli threw himself down, his face in his hands, and sobbed, "My strength is gone from me, my brothers. I hear things behind me, but no one's there. I lie down, but can't rest. I run, but don't feel any better. I bathe, but don't cool my body. I was always strong, but my bones now feel like water. What has happened to me?"

"Your body is telling you it's time to go back to your life as a man," said old Baloo. "You never listened when Akela said you should, or even when I said it. Bagheera knows it too, wherever he is tonight."

"And I knew it when we met at the Cold Lairs," added Kaa. "Man must go to Man even though the jungle doesn't cast him out."

The Four Brothers nodded to each other, then to their little brother.

"The jungle isn't c-c-casting me out then?" stammered Mowgli in surprise.

The Four growled furiously, "As long as we live, no one shall dare—"

But Baloo interrupted them. "I taught you the Law of the Jungle, Little Brother, so I

"It's Time to Go Back."

should be the one to speak. Even though I can barely see the rocks in front of me, I can see far off. You must follow your own trail. You must make your home with your own people. But remember, if you ever need any of us, our eyes, our teeth, our feet, our wings to carry messages, our Jungle-People will always be yours to command."

"Oh, my brothers!" sobbed Mowgli, flinging his arms up toward the sky. "I don't want to leave you, but my feet are pulling me away."

"It's nothing to be ashamed of," said the old bear. "When our honey is gone, we leave the hive. It's the Law of the Jungle."

"And when we shed our skin, we don't crawl back into it," said Kaa. "It's the Law too."

"Listen, dearest child," reassured Baloo, "there's nothing here in the jungle for you, nothing to hold you here. You're not a man-cub asking for permission to leave his pack. You're the master of the jungle who's going off on a new trail. No one can dispute that!"

"Oh, My Brothers!"

"But Bagheera and the bull that bought—"

Mowgli's words were cut short by a roar and a crash in the bushes below the Rock. Then Bagheera appeared, announcing, "I've just finished a long hunt, Little Brother, and a bull lies dead in the bushes. Just as a bull once bought you, now this bull frees you." And he bounded away down the hill.

Bagheera stopped at the foot of the hill and called out, long and loud, "Good hunting on your new trail, master of the jungle! Remember, Bagheera loved you!"

"Now you've heard it from us all, Little Frog," said Baloo. "Come into my arms."

Mowgli threw his arms around the blind bear's neck and sobbed and sobbed.

"It's hard casting off your skin of childhood," said Kaa, "but on your new trail, you will grow into your skin of manhood!"

"And we Four must follow our own new wolf trails as well," said Gray Brother. "For Man goes to Man at last!"

"Remember, Bagheera Loved You!"